# CYNTHIA RYLANT

# POPPLETON
## IN WINTER

### BOOK EIGHT

*Illustrated by*
# MARK TEAGUE

SCHOLASTIC INC.
New York Toronto London Auckland Sydney
Mexico City New Delhi Hong Kong Buenos Aires

*For Boris*
C. R.

*For Laura*
M. T.

This book is being published simultaneously in hardcover
by the Blue Sky Press.

ISBN 0-590-84838-0

Text copyright © 2001 by Cynthia Rylant
Illustrations copyright © 2001 by Mark Teague
All rights reserved.
Published by Scholastic Inc.
SCHOLASTIC and associated logos are trademarks and/or
registered trademarks of Scholastic Inc.

12 11 10 9 8 7 6 5          2 3 4 5 6/0

Printed in the United States of America          23

Designed by Kathleen Westray

First Scholastic paperback printing, October 2001

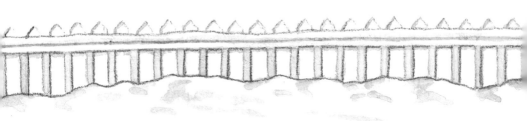

# CONTENTS

# ICICLES

Poppleton's house grew
very long icicles in winter.

Poppleton was proud of them.

He never knocked them down.

He just let them get longer and longer.

Gus, the mail carrier, said,
"Poppleton, you should do
something about those icicles."

Hudson down the street said,
"Poppleton, those icicles
are *not pretty*!"

And when Poppleton's mother visited,
she said that an icicle was surely
going to bonk him on the head.

But Poppleton didn't listen to any of them.

He loved his icicles.

Each morning he took a ruler outside

to see how much longer they had grown.

Then one day a little finch wasn't
watching where he was going.
He ran into *one* icicle.
And that one fell into
the next one which fell into
the next one which fell into
the next one.

And soon all of Poppleton's icicles
were lying on the ground.
Poppleton was sad.
The little finch felt so bad.
"I'm very sorry," he said.
"It's all right," Poppleton said politely.

"Maybe we could build something
with them," said the finch.

"Build something?" asked Poppleton.

"Sure," said the finch. "The icicles
are still frozen. We could make them
into something."

Poppleton and the finch
worked all day long.

And by evening, Poppleton had the most beautiful picket fence in town!

"Would you like to stay for dinner?"
Poppleton asked the finch (whose
name was Patrick).

"Certainly!" said Patrick.

Poppleton was glad his icicles

were knocked down.

Icicles always melted.

But a new friend would stay.

# THE BUST

Winter always made Poppleton creative.
One winter he built a pagoda
out of ice-cream sticks.

Another winter he hooked a rug.
Another winter he painted stars
on all his floors.

Now it was time to be creative again.

*What shall I make this winter?*
Poppleton thought.

He looked out his window and saw
Cherry Sue in her house.

"I know!" said Poppleton. "I'll make
a bust of Cherry Sue!"
Poppleton went to the art store
and bought some clay.

Then he started molding
Cherry Sue's head.

"Hmmm. I can't remember what Cherry Sue's hair looks like," said Poppleton.

He walked over to Cherry Sue's
and knocked on the door.
"Hello, Poppleton," said Cherry Sue.
"Hello!" said Poppleton.

"Come in," said Cherry Sue.

"No thanks. I just wanted
to say hello," said Poppleton,
looking closely at her head.

He went back home and started molding.

"Hmmm," said Poppleton.

"I can't remember what Cherry Sue's

eyes look like."

He walked over to Cherry Sue's
and knocked on the door.

"Yes?" said Cherry Sue.
Poppleton looked deeply into
Cherry Sue's eyes.
"Nice to see you. Good-bye,"
said Poppleton.

He went back home and
started molding.

"Hmmm," said Poppleton. "I can't
remember what Cherry Sue's
nose looks like."

He walked over to Cherry Sue's
and knocked on the door.
"You again," said Cherry Sue.
Poppleton stared at her nose.

She tweaked his.

"Ow!" said Poppleton. "You tweaked my nose!"

"Because you're making me crazy!" said Cherry Sue.

"I'm only trying to make a bust
of your head!" said Poppleton.

"Really?" Cherry Sue said.

"I can't remember what you look like,"
Poppleton said, rubbing his nose.

"I'll get my coat," said Cherry Sue.

She followed Poppleton back
to his house.

She sat very still while he molded.

It took five hours.

But when the bust was done,
it looked just like Cherry Sue.

"Sorry I tweaked your nose,"
she told Poppleton.

And she gave it a little kiss.

# THE SLEIGH RIDE

It was a very snowy day and
Poppleton felt like a sleigh ride.
He called his friend Cherry Sue.

"Would you like to go for a sleigh ride?"
Poppleton asked.
"Sorry, Poppleton, I'm making
cookies," said Cherry Sue.

Poppleton called his friend Hudson.

"Would you like to go for a sleigh ride?"
Poppleton asked.

"Sorry," said Hudson,

"I'm baking a cake."

Poppleton called his friend Fillmore.

"Would you like to go for a sleigh ride?"
Poppleton asked.

"Sorry," said Fillmore.

"I'm stirring some fudge."

Poppleton was so disappointed.

He couldn't find one friend for a sleigh ride.

And besides that, they were all making

such good things to eat!

He sat in front of his window,
feeling very sorry for himself.
Suddenly the doorbell rang.

"SURPRISE!"

There stood all of Poppleton's friends! With cookies and cake and fudge and presents!

"HAPPY BIRTHDAY, POPPLETON!"

He had forgotten his own birthday!
Everyone ate and laughed and played
games with Poppleton.

Then, just before midnight,
they all took him on a sleigh ride.

The moon was full and white.

The stars twinkled.

The owls hooted in the trees.

Over the snow went the sleigh filled

with Poppleton and all of his friends.

Poppleton didn't even make
a birthday wish.
He had everything already.

POTATO CLAUS: Ho Ho Ho! Potato Claus loves you too! I will see you next year!

THE END

POTATO CLAUS: Here are small bags of
potato chips for everyone. And now,
goodbye!

EVERYONE: Goodbye, Potato Claus!
We love you!

ELVIS AND FRANCESCA: Potato Claus! We love you!

ELVIS: Oh, Francesca! Look at all the wonderful gifts in Potato Claus's Great Book. I choose the potato skates!

FRANCESCA: And I choose the potato-cycle!

POTATO CLAUS: And you shall have them! They will be delivered to you by Unified Parcel Service in seven to ten working days.

Potato-cycle

Potato skate

POTATO CLAUS: It makes no difference to me if they have been good or not good. Potato Claus does not judge. Ho Ho Ho!

POTATO CLAUS: Mr. and Mrs. Creamedcorn, may little Elvis and Francesca choose gifts from my book?

MR. CREAMEDCORN: Yes, Potato Claus. They have been good children, and they deserve gifts.

POTATO CLAUS: Ho Ho Ho! I have no time to enjoy potato pancakes with you, Mrs. Creamedcorn. I must visit many homes with the Great Book of Gifts.

ELVIS AND FRANCESCA: Ohhh! The Great Book of Gifts! The Great Book of Gifts!

MR. CREAMEDCORN: Welcome to our house, Potato Claus, friend to children everywhere.

MRS. CREAMEDCORN: Please join us in a meal of holiday potato pancakes, Potato Claus.

FRANCESCA: Mother! Father! Dear brother Elvis! See who is here! It is Potato Claus, loved by children all over the world.

POTATO CLAUS: Ho Ho Ho! Happy Christmas, Kwanzaa, Chanukah, Winter Solstice, and also local and regional winter holidays and celebrations! Ho Ho Ho!

# A Visit From Potato Claus
## A Play
### by Bob and Gloria

It is a winter's day in the home of Mr. and Mrs. Creamedcorn, who are both astronauts. Their lovely children, Elvis and Francesca, are doing their homework. Mrs. Creamedcorn is making potato pancakes. The doorbell rings.

ELVIS: There is someone at the door.

FRANCESCA: I will see who it is.

Francesca opens the door, and we see it is Potato Claus, loved by children all over the world.

"We have already chosen the actors," Big
Gloria said. "Tina Tiny will play the mother.
Billy Thimble will play the father. Big Bob
and myself will play Elvis and Francesca,
who are the children. And you, Mr. Salami,
will play the part of Potato Claus."

# We Get Ready

"Writing the play is just the first part," Mr. Salami said. "Now we have to choose the actors. Then we have to practice. Then we put on the play in front of the class."

We took the play to school the next day. We showed it to Mr. Salami.

"This is good!" Mr. Salami said.